1.25

THINGS I LIKE ABOUT GRANDMA

She hugs me good.
She's always glad to see me.
She makes every day special!

DEDICATION

For some very special grandmothers — for Nana (my mother) and Aunt Lacothia;
and in memory of Aunt Lawrencie, my grandmothers Nora Datcher and
Gertrude Haskins, and my dear friend Lillian Downs.
And for all the grandmothers who are now raising their grandchildren.
Francine Haskins

Story and pictures copyright (c) 1992 by Francine Haskins.   All rights reserved.
Editors: Harriet Rohmer and David Schecter   Design: Mira Reisberg   Production: Tony Yuen   Photography: Lee Fatherree
Printed in Hong Kong through Interprint.   Children's Book Press is a nonprofit community publisher.
Children's Book Press is grateful to the California Arts Council, the Wallace Alexander Gerbode Foundation, the Fleishacker Foundation,
the Wells Fargo Foundation, and the Neutrogena Corporation whose generous donations helped support
the publication of THINGS I LIKE ABOUT GRANDMA through our "Books About You and Me" project.

Library of Congress Cataloging-in-Publication Data
Haskins, Francine.   Things I like about Grandma / Francine Haskins.   p. cm.
Summary: An African American girl tells of her close relationship with her grandmother.   ISBN 0-89239-107-3
[1. Grandmothers—Fiction. 2. African Americans—Fiction.]   I. Title. PZ7.H2763Th 1992 [Fic]—dc20 92-16305 CIP AC

Children's Book Press   San Francisco and Emeryville, California

THINGS I LIKE ABOUT GRANDMA

Francine Haskins

I like Grandma because she tells me stories of the "old days" — stories about Africa, about the slaves, about how things used to be, and stories about Mommy when she was a little girl like me. She even has pictures!

I help Grandma make her beautiful quilts. They tell a story of our family. She lets me thread her needles and pick out the patches.

Grandma has lots and lots of plants. She has a "green thumb." She lets me help her plant flowers and vegetables in her back yard. My job is to water the flowers and try to stay dry. (smile)

Saturday afternoon my grandma likes to bake her "goodies." She lets me help her mix the batter and lick the bowl clean when we are finished!

Every Sunday Grandma takes me to Sunday school, then she goes to church. After church she and her friends always stop and chat and say to me, "My, you certainly are getting to be a big girl!" I smile.

Grandma and I take
homemade cookies
and cakes with
us when we go

to visit her friends at Banneker House, the senior citizens' home.

They play cards and talk about the "old days." Sometimes they look sad. I sit in my chair with my crayons and coloring book and listen.

I like to go to the grocery store with Grandma. I help her push the cart and carry her groceries. If I'm good she lets me have a treat from the bakery.

We go to the cleaners,
post office and hardware store. Everybody
says "hello" to Grandma. They think she's special. So do I!

When Grandma gets her social security check, she rides the bus

downtown
to the bank. Sometimes
I go with her. Grandma only pays
half fare and we get to sit in the priority
seating for senior citizens. I watch the people.

While we are downtown, we have our special lunch — bacon, lettuce and tomato sandwich and hot coffee.

When Grandma goes to her neighborhood hairdresser, I like to watch Miss Carolyn turn Grandma's hair blue, press it and curl it. The ladies laugh and gossip and listen to gospel music.

Before Grandma combs my hair she lets
me try on her wig and earrings.
I pretend I'm Grandma.
We laugh and
have fun!

I like Grandma because she does "boy things" too, like watching the football game on TV with Granddaddy. I really like Grandma because she makes every day special!

A NOTE FROM THE AUTHOR/ARTIST

THINGS I LIKE ABOUT GRANDMA
is about the relationship between grandmother and granddaughter. It's a special relationship. It's teaching, telling, giving, and bonding. It's learning family histories and traditions, things that have been passed from generation to generation. It's building the foundation — giving the child a basis to grow on and come back to. It's love shared.

Francine Haskins

Francine Haskins is a celebrated artist, dollmaker, teacher, and storyteller living in Washington, D.C. Her first book with Children's Book Press, I REMEMBER "121," is a loving portrait of her family and her childhood in Washington's African American community.